That's Rich
By
Richard Palmer

First Printing 2020

ISBN 978-0-9525494-5-1

Published by
Richard Palmer
Cover Design by John Goodwin.

Illustrations Public Domain

That's Rich

Acknowledgements

I would like to thank my wife Linda for sharing my life and frustrations in producing this book and my first book, 'Rich Inspirations' Promiscuous poems and Twisted tales. Without her help, understanding, patience and computer knowledge it would still be a pile of papers.

Thanks to the members of Paphos Writers Group for help, encouragement and feedback, each week for the past six years.

A special thanks to my friend and fellow writer John Goodwin of Anixe Publishing Ltd. for his help in publishing this book.

Thanks to brother Dave (Fred) for encouragement and being my brother and for leaving us with many happy memories. Also my grandson Christopher Palmer for his technical support.

Thanks to friends Martin and Sally Walker, David and Carolyn Hart, Peter Bruce and Carole Richards, Chris King and Vicky Mills plus many more who have endured my ramblings and given their views, often while enjoying a few cool drinks at Yialos Tavern, Coral Bay, Cyprus.

Richard Palmer

That's Rich

Contents

8

That's Rich

1) THE TEARJERKER

What's up duck, said the little kitten

I don't really know; I think I've been smitten

You see, my mum got killed, hit by a car

Left me all alone to waddle oh so far

My brothers and sisters were all I had

But they never crossed the motorway, it was all very sad

The lorry never stopped; the driver unaware

And other motorists hit them but didn't seem to care

I waddled and waddled for many a mile

Then totally exhausted, I saw you and your smile

You purred and purred as I got very near

Then you stretched out a paw and meowed, 'duck, come here'

You gave me a cuddle, held me warm and tight

Found us some shelter, where we spent the night

Two total strangers brought together by fate

'Yes I am smitten, for now and forever you're my special mate.

2) THE QUESTIONABLE KID

'Mummy.'

'Yes dear.'

'Uncle Tobie said he is a Roadie.'

'That's right dear.'

'Mummy.'

'Yes dear.'

'What is a Roadie?'

'It is someone who looks after a band.'

'Mummy.'

'Yes dear.'

'What is a band?'

'It is four or five people who sing, play guitars and drums.'

'Mummy.

'Yes dear.'

'What is a guitar?'

'It is a musical instrument dear.'

'Mummy.'

'Yes dear.'

'How do you play it?'

'By plucking with a plectrum dear.'

'Mummy.'

'Yes dear.'

'What is a flectrum?'

'No darling, the word is plectrum not flectrum.'

'Mummy.'

'Yes dear.'

'What is flucking?'

'No dear, the word is plucking.'

'Mummy.'

'Yes dear.'

'I heard uncle Tobie say Rick from the band could not play the guitar.'

'Rick can play the guitar dear, in fact he is one of the best guitarists around.'

'Mummy.'

'Yes dear.'

'I have learnt to say plectrum.'

'That's good, who taught you?'

'No one, but I heard Rick from the band say he could not play the guitar because there was no 'effin plectrum.'

3) TERROR AND FEAR

Pension day at last, Gladys Hewson, an eighty two year old ex postmistress had been having a very difficult time since her husband Harry had passed away a few years ago. They had rented a house all their lives but due to rising costs she had been forced to move in with her granddaughter and husband Michael. Not ideal but their twin boys aged four gave her plenty of company and amusement. As they were not yet attending full time school, Gladys made an ideal babysitter while their parents were at work. She also got time to relax when they were at pre-school and later she would collect them which brought back many happy memories of her own children. The twins were often very boisterous and untidy in the house but she got used to their ways and was thankful to be able to enjoy and share their lives.

After dropping them off at pre-school, she made her way to the post office to collect her pension. 'Good morning Mary,' she said with a smile as the postmistress greeted her. 'These pension payment days seem to take a long time to come these days,' said Gladys. The two young men at the counter with hoods covering most of their features, gestured for her to be served first. Nice to see some manners, she thought as she pushed the cash into her purse. She slowly walked the short distance to the house but became uneasy as the two men from the post office walked slightly behind her on the opposite pavement. She entered the house, placing her handbag and purse on the table. After a nice cup of tea she fell asleep on the settee.

Some time later she woke to the sound of the front door slamming. Before she had time to move from her deep slumber, two masked males burst through the lounge doorway, each pushing a gun into her face. She froze with terror and fear. Her pension money seemed insignificant as she became aware that her life was in serious danger. A voice from the kitchen eased the look of terror on her face as her granddaughter shouted, 'Gran, I picked the twins up from school and took them shopping for cowboy outfits, hope they are not bothering you too much in there.'

4) A BLUE BLOODED BABY

My name is 'Archie' and I've got Royal blood

I don't know if that's bad or if it's very good

I've only just been born and I'm famous far and wide

Thanks to my dad Harry whose heart is full of pride

My mum's a mass of smiles, as radiant as can be

She is so delighted to have given birth to little ol' me

Apparently I am blessed to have blood so pure and blue

But little did I know, it's also the colour of my poo

It makes me feel contented and very, very happy

Especially when I fart and fill my Royal nappy

My grandad thinks I'm cute, Charlie is his name

He's got Royal blood, so I think we're much the same

Except I am very young and he is very old

Married to Camilla, a nice lady I am told

It's sad my grandma died, so beautiful with grace

She would have glowed as she looked upon my face

But it was not to be, it was time for her to go

And now that I am born, she is someone I'll never know

So what of the future, I'll never see the throne

Unless I'm in the bathroom sitting all alone

But I'll never have to worry, I'll never have to rush

And when I've done my duty, I'll give a Royal flush

So to all you lovely people who love my mum and dad

Share your life with me because I think it won't be bad.

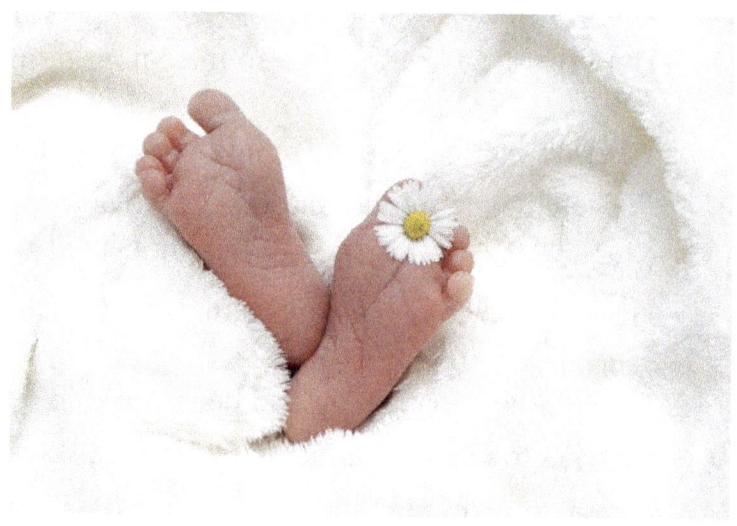

5) I COULDN'T BELIEVE MY EYES

We can all dream and I dreamed big. As a cleaner in a factory, there had to be more to life. The rent and bills for my two bedroom flat in an undesirable part of town were crippling on my wages and my eighteen year old drop out, pot smoking, useless son only added to my woes. He had never done a day's work since leaving school at fifteen, he mixed with a bad crowd and spent his dole money on dope and booze and just lazed around all day. I tried so hard to get him motivated but in the end I just gave up in frustration.

My only satisfaction in life is writing. It takes me out of my miserable existence and puts me in a fantasy world of love, passion, wealth and exciting adventures. I had been writing a thriller fiction novel for about three years, there was just the final chapter to complete but the twist at the end had eluded me for some time. Naturally I had dreams of it being a world best seller along with thousands of other budding authors, why not, it was all part of my fantasy land.

One day I returned home from work as a cleaner to find my flat trashed, my treasured personal items, mementos, photographs of my parents, long departed, torn to shreds. My childhood memories obliterated except in my mind. I burst into tears, the knowledge of being burgled was bad enough but then the full horror hit me. My lifeline, my laptop with my book encased in its depths along with the paper version and backup memory stick, all gone. I collapsed in a heap onto the computer chair, the thought of having to start all over again was unimaginable. My whole life for what it is had just caved in, it was though a big part of me had died. The huge row with my son the night before had already upset me, I told him to sort himself out, get a job or get out. No! No! I thought, he wouldn't, then I found the scrawled note which read, 'sick of this shit life and your moaning, gone to find a better one. I was distraught, he was useless but he was still my son. I tried his mobile, dead. Over the following weeks I contacted his friends, no one had seen or heard from him. I reported him missing but after a couple of months the dole office stopped paying out, now there was no trace. My mind became numb and vacant, which was the greatest loss, my son having gone off or my dream book, I didn't know but both felt like a loss through death

I struggled on with my life, I left the factory and now worked in a hospital as an auxiliary nurse. I thought, if my dreams have gone I can help others with theirs.

One afternoon about three years later, I was attending to an elderly lady at the hospital, I asked what she was reading, she handed me the book. I did not recognise the title, I began to read, shock went through my body, I couldn't believe what I was seeing. I flicked through the pages, this was my book, my story, three years of dreams, frustrations, re writing, editing, exasperation, it was all here in my hand. 'Can I borrow your book,' I asked. 'Of course my dear,' she replied. During my break I sat in the rest room and went straight for the last chapter, again I could not believe my eyes. The one thing that had eluded me was now complete and brilliantly written.

That night I was up till the early hours going through every page. It was just as I had written it apart from the last chapter. The following day I contacted the publishers. The book was a world best seller and film rights had been sold. There was a package for me, they would send a courier. Later that week on my day off, a prestige car pulled up and there was a knock at the door, the courier hopefully I thought, but on opening it, there stood my son, smartly dressed, with a beaming smile. We hugged hard and as he came in he handed over a package. I was shocked but excited, as there in my hand was the authenticated publishing and film rights to my book, in my name which had made millions. 'Who, what, why,' I asked. 'Does it matter, just sign it, I love you mum.'

6 MAN'S BEST FRIEND.

Its been seventeen years since I first found you

Tossed In a skip, in a box with an old shoe

Three weeks old, weak and distraught

I fought through the rubble, a life to save as I was taught

I took you home, gave you food, love and care

You responded with affection as I stroked your hair

You grew so strong and became my best friend

And we shared our lives right to the end

Walks in the park in the early morning light

Then a run through the woods before the dark of night

A whimpering of love and a wagging tail

Was my reward from a friend once frail

Our bond was so strong, I would have given you my life

To save you from cruelty, misery and strife

Each day after work as I returned home

You were always there along with your bone

But one day I was kept rather late

And found it strange you were not by the gate

I searched around calling your name

But you were nowhere to be seen in the country lane

Eventually I found you tossed in a skip

Hit by a car where the road did dip

Your body mangled, oozing blood

The end of a friendship that was so good

I took you home and in my garden you now lay

As I'm left with memories of my best friend, each and every day.

7) WHAT IF.

What if at age 62, I phone the dating agency and they reject me.

What if no one wants me.

What if I book a restaurant and she doesn't turn up?

What if she is ugly and fat with spots?

What if she has facial hair?

What if she is blind with a stick?

What if she is deaf and dumb?

What if she is pregnant?

What if she is over 90 and frail?

What if she brings her 6 kids with her?

What if she's in a wheelchair?

What if she is Dianne Abbott or Gemma Collins?

What if she can't speak English?

What if she's a drug addict or alcoholic?

What if she doesn't like my stutter?

What if she doesn't understand my accent?

What if she's a porn star and a nymphomaniac?

What if she is beautiful but underage?

What if she is rich and glamorous?

What if she's a film star?

What if she is a Lady or Countess?

I waited nervously, a hand tapped me on the shoulder,

'You Pete,'

'Yes I replied.' I turned round to be greeted by my date, ugly, big and loud.

'A' right mate, my names 'Arry.'

8) FAMILY BOTHER

'Margaret, it's Dwayne in the U.K, how are you.'

'Wow, this is a surprise, she exclaimed, yes, I am fine.'

'And the rest of the family.'

'Yes, all fine.'

'Seen anything of my wayward brother recently.'

'Not for a few months but I am sure he is okay, otherwise he would be in touch, usually does if there is a problem.'

'What about Sheila, she okay?.

'Yes Sheila is fine, recently moved to Adelaide but we meet up now and then, her and Harry came for tea a few weeks ago, 'they will be surprised when I tell them you have been in touch, how long has it been?'

'A few years, been very busy with the business and Dad.'

'How is the grumpy old bugger, not spoken to him since he divorced Mum.'

'Well, that's why I am ringing, I know none of the family in Australia have had much to do with him over the years but he is still their father.'

'Why, what's up,' Margaret queried with a hint of anxiety in her voice.

'Sorry to have to say this Margaret, but he passed away on Friday.'

'Oh my God,' she shrieked, 'what happened, what did he die of'?

'Heart attack, went out like a light.'

'Oh dear, that's sad even though we despised him at times, it brings it home, he was our father.'

'What's going to happen, we are all miles away here in Australia, said Margaret with emotion now building inside her.

'Well the funeral will be in a weeks' time, then the solicitor will sort out the will, no idea what's involved, as you know, Dad owned a few houses which are rented out and he had plenty of money, not that he ever mentioned it, wouldn't even help me out when the business got in a mess . . . Anyway, there lies the problem, I am so strapped for cash I can't afford to pay for his funeral and solicitors' costs and wondered if you and the family could help. I know you are all in the will, to what extent I do not know, not until it is read.'

'Well, we are not wealthy but can manage that between us,' said Margaret, but there is no way we can get there for the funeral, Bob's away on business and I am due in hospital on Thursday for an operation, have been waiting a long time due to complications with my blood and I can't miss it.'

'What about the others,' he asked.

'I can ask but can't see them coming, they hated him for what he did, will or no will.'

'Well I can sort everything out and get the solicitor to forward all the necessary papers to you and he will inform you of the contents of the will but I will need the cost of the funeral as the will may take a bit longer.'

'Tell me how much you need and we will forward it to your bank,' said Margaret.

'I know I shouldn't do this to family but I am desperate, in a few days I can sort out my financial problems.' He got the money and a couple of months later but had still not been in touch with the family. He ignored their calls. A few weeks later he answered a local call, it was Margaret.

'You lying, cheating load of crap Dwayne.'

'I'm sorry, Margaret, how did you find out.'

'Because Dad phoned me and right now we are having a drink in your local pub, we will be round very soon.

9) MIND OVER MATTER

Eighty one years I have been on this Earth and there has not, as far as I know, been a time when you have not been there. You guided me through a turbulent life, from a baby, although like most people, there are no recollections from those days, probably about aged three would be the norm. Later you were there on my first day at school, we listened and studied together and over time we gained amazing knowledge and intelligence, not just academically but about life. We were inseparable and put great trust in each other as we shared a special bond full of love, sadness, happiness, pain and so much emotion as we laughed and cried.

My first bike ride, swimming lessons, the day I got lost, the first kiss while holding hands in the back row of the cinema and eventually my first sexual encounter. It was you who gave me strength and wisdom to carry out these tasks. On one occasion while partying with friends, I got totally drunk on vodka and fell flat on the floor with my friends standing around me laughing. Suddenly you were not there to help me and I was useless and incapable on my own. I woke up in bed the following morning and you were there, but neither me or you were of any use to each other. I was limp and fragile and you were totally mixed up, almost delirious. It wasn't until the next morning that we were able to connect with each other and make some sense as to what had gone on. The worrying thing was that my knickers were in my handbag, no wonder I had a crowd round me. Were you bothered, not one jot, anything could have happened in my moments of total abandonment. It was like the time I lost my virginity at sixteen, a bit young but you were well up for it even though my pure untouched body was not. Go for it, go for it, that's all I got out of you. I would have sat there like a dummy but suddenly I am laying there, legs wide open screaming in pure ecstasy, and why, because you interfered and urged me on. I felt degraded afterwards and hated you, for I was no longer a pure innocent girl. Later on, again with your encouragement, because I had done it once, I might as well carry on. You just didn't seem to care and I just went along for the ride, so to speak. Anyway, as you know, I got pregnant and the real bond and understanding really kicked in. There were some major decisions to be made like abortion, adoption, the possibility of my body being cut open for a caesarean operation, also the stigma of being a young unmarried mother and the effect it would have on my family. I must admit, in the end you were magnificent, you gave me the strength to carry on and make the right decision.

My son has been amazing, although at times I had my doubts. A handsome grown up man now, university educated, chairman of his own successful company. I sometimes wonder what I would have done without him, he may be married with my two lovely grandchildren who visit me now and then but he makes sure I have everything I need, love and affection, financial security, home comforts and all the care and attention I could hope for in this superior nursing home.

These days I no longer write my thoughts and memories down, for you are no longer there to guide me. You are somewhere deep in my brain, gone but not totally forgotten. Life can be cruel when you have lost your mind to dementia.

That's Rich

10) AN ALTERNATIVE CHRISTMAS

Snowflakes glistened as they fell to the ground
An eerie morning, hardly a sound
A rustle of leaves, the tweet of a bird
Apart from that, nothing was heard

The sun was fighting to shine through the grey
To make things happen on Amazon day
It used to have meaning, a belief of some kind
But religious fanatics had it refined

Words were taboo, beliefs soon forgot
As children were brainwashed straight from the cot
Believing in nothing but the power of greed
Set in their minds like a flourishing seed

The special list of toys they desire
Used to lay by the extinct coal fire
With a puff of soot his bag he led
Then laid the toys on their bed

But in modern times all this has gone
As they wait for the post from Amazon
Computers, X boxes, games galore
Sadly the magic is no more.

11) TRAPPED

It was a new world, a new life, a new adventure and a place of great opportunity for the young attractive girl brought up in the lush countryside of South Georgia. She had led a quiet and sheltered life on her parents' farm, away from the hustle and bustle of towns. Being shy, she seldom entered into conversation with others, restricting her thoughts and ideas to a couple of close friends who could often be found in a quiet area of the local park.

Like most young girls of seventeen, they talked of boyfriends, fashion, pop stars and the glamorous life that the world media put into their minds. She had never been to a major city and although the thought of going was daunting, it was also very exciting. Her parents were not happy with her leaving the family home but they gave their blessing, realising their daughter had grown up and wished to follow her dreams.

Being a budding writer, she accomplished her dream of becoming a reporter by securing a job with a national newspaper. Although only a junior, she worked hard and showed lots of promise which was noticed by her superiors. After a period of probation she was sent out to report on minor events.

To her, New York city was a fantasy land compared to her upbringing. Life was fast and furious and it took a few years for her to adapt and become the confident person and reporter she now portrayed. Naturally like all journalists, she had dreams of finding a big story that would either shock or inspire the world, where, when or if ever it would happen, no one knew but the thought of it kept her excited mind alive with exhilaration.

Her reporting abilities and devotion and loyalty to her job was most welcomed by her employers who rewarded her with more interesting and important topics. The once shy girl was now interviewing important people, mayors, law and fire officers, sheriffs, the odd congressman, all dealing with disputes and disasters which the community wanted to know about. She was happy in her role but still had the burning desire to find the 'big' story.

A few days holiday came up and she decided to have some fun and let her hair down. An invite to a 'jet set' party in the Presidential suite of the five star Manhattan Hotel came her way, she thought, *why not, it could be very interesting and entertaining.*

That evening, dressed to look like a beautiful princess, she entered the Presidential suite on the thirty second floor of one of the most influential hotels in New York. To say it was plush was an understatement, the scent of power and money was abundant. Eyes gazed at her as alone, she slowly made her way across the room. It did not take long before a drink was in her hand and several dapper gentlemen were by her side eager to make her acquaintance.

As the night progressed and the party moved past midnight, she strolled onto a balcony to take in the sights and cool fresh air. A charming handsome young man appeared, they began to chat and after a while she could feel a chemistry between them. Suddenly, there was a tremendous explosion a few floors below, she screamed in fear.

They looked down as flames burst through shattered windows, shards of glass could be seen glistening in the orange glow assisted by the bright moon. Another explosion came, in sheer panic she grabbed her new acquaintance with both hands, fiercely hugging him tightly. The flames rose towards them, they moved to the balcony door, it had automatically locked, there was no escape, they were trapped. The whole of the top floors were now an inferno, the heat was intense, any moment now they would be burnt alive. In total fear she kissed and kissed the young man, taking breaths to scream. 'I forgot your name,' he said.

'It's Lois, Lois Lane and your name is . . .'

12) WHEN I WAS A CHILD

When I was a child I used to play and have fun

From early morning until the setting sun

With my mates I felt safe and very secure

As we ran through the countryside and over the moor

No one to bother us, no one to complain

No one to shout or call out our name

Strangers said 'hello,' we smiled while passing by

We lived in a haven of love, never shy

We had no fear as there was no threat

As violence and crime had not reached us yet

But as time passed by, we moved to a city

Where homeless beggars asked for your pity

No hope in life, no reason to live

No feeling of love, nothing to give

Crime was rife, drugs were the core

As addicts craved for more and more

Houses were robbed, people were shot

As druggies made sure a fix they got

People responded and bought a gun

And it was plain to see it wasn't for fun

To protect his children, property and wife

He shot the intruders ending their life

But decades later everyone has a gun

And the lack of control had begun

Mass shootings are now commonplace

With no regard to life of the human race

There is no cure, there is no solution

America is riddled with gun pollution

13) THE DIMWITTED TERRORIST

Mohamed Mohsen is the Islamic Commander of the People's Revolutionary Army against Western infidels and democracy. His brother, Mohamed Morsil had been sentenced to twenty five years in jail for terrorist crimes. His brother vowed revenge and organised a plan to kill politicians and many world leaders who would be meeting for a conference on world affairs at 1pm in the Houses of Parliament.

After creating a diversion by means of a bomb scare, Mohamed and his small band of men, entered the grounds in the dark the previous evening and hid in a disused coal shed. The following day they forced a window and entered Parliament disguised as Arab Politicians. At 12.55.pm, armed with automatic weapons, they burst into the conference room after overpowering the security guards.

They stood in silence for a few moments, staring into the room. There were no Politicians, World Leaders or anyone in a suit, just cleaners and staff arranging the room. They quickly made their escape into the grounds and hid in the bushes. Suddenly, Big Ben struck a note, 1 pm thought Mohamed, but no, another note was struck and another, eventually it struck 12.00 noon. Mohamed stared at the clock, a little bewildered. They discarded the weapons and robes and made their way to a bench in the park opposite, where they sat as not to cause suspicion. Mohamed picked up a discarded newspaper from the day before, the headlines read, 'Don't forget to put your clocks back at midnight tonight.'

14) THERE'S NO PLACE LIKE HOME

Nigel Marmaduke Forsythe smiled as he gazed out across the lavish extensive grounds of the imposing stately home which had been in the family for over two hundred years. His eyes focussed on the acres of forest surrounding the huge lake with its fountains, the summerhouse and veranda where many a tea party had been held by Lords and Ladies over the decades. Even though the place had a historic and colourful recorded history, he wondered about all the past intriguing stories and events that had occurred amongst the local gentry. The flirtations and sexual encounters in the woods that they were renowned for despite their status and the following consequences they and their families had to deal with. Family shame, divorce, pregnancies, gay encounters which were kept highly secret, it all sounded exciting to Nigel who was an avid writer of life in the past.

On reaching the far end of the lake, he looked back towards the house and thought how things had changed even though the grounds had remained much the same. The metallic blue Rolls Royce and the salmon pink Porsche with their electric hoods down in the bright sunshine revealing fine leather seats, stood where the once exquisite high quality coaches and white horses waited with their footmen to transport the owners and guests to and from their homes. How things have progressed thought Nigel, but he was very grateful to have all this in his life, to write about it and share with others.

He decided to stroll up the hill through the lush grass field with its multitude of buttercups and a few oak and horse-chestnut trees towering over them. The smell of spring was in the air and Nigel felt good and grateful to be a part of the magical nature that was life. Having served eight years in the army as a Captain in the Royal Artillery, Nigel had become a more humble person having lost a leg to an I.E.D in war torn Afghanistan where he was awarded the George medal for saving the lives of several of his comrades while risking his own life. After months of operations and skin grafts followed by physiotherapy and pain management, plus the fitting of prosthetic limbs, Nigel returned to his hometown having been discharged from the Army. He stayed with close friends who cared for him. Unable to drive or walk far, he requested that they take him to see his beloved stately home. He stayed in the car, his eyes soaking up the beautiful surroundings, this was his place of inspirations and dreams, the background to his writing.

A year later his friends split up and divorced, selling their home and leaving Nigel to his own devices. He was more agile now and able to do things for himself. He returned to the stately home and all the memories of the time he had spent there came flooding back. He wandered and sat among the buttercups in the field on the hillside, reflecting on his life. He slowly strolled to the village high street; the recessed large oak double doors of his new abode greeted him with a marble pillar each side. Darkness had arrived as he rested his weary and tired body, he lay on his back gazing skyward and through a small hole in the top of his one man nylon tent he could see several twinkling stars in the clear sky. He buried himself deep into his warm sleeping bag, his binoculars safely by his side. A couple of tots of rum found in a rubbish bin gave him a warm sensation as he closed his eyes. I wonder what tomorrow will bring, he thought, may go and sit among the buttercups and look at that stately home again, in the meantime, it's good to be back, there's no place like home.

15) GONE BUT NOT FORGOTTEN

I remember the seventies so full of flair
With wide bottom trousers and masses of hair
I was sharp as a button and could see for miles
And people remarked on my magical smiles
Fitness and health were my main concern
And a marathon run with calories to burn
Skin like a baby's, torso so sleek
As my muscles got stronger week after week
Health food and pills, not a beer touched my lips
As I built up strength in my stomach and hips
Smoking was out and so was the pub
No chips or burgers, just protein grub
No late night parties or whisky and rum
Just an early night and a morning run
So what happened to me, you may say
As decades later, on the couch I lay
Bald as a coot, blind as a bat
No masses of hair, just a flat cap
No cause for a smile with my wrinkly skin
Surrounded by fast food fit for the bin
Flab on my arms, obese in the gut
Arthritic legs and gout in the foot

No jogging for me as I lay on the couch
Drinking beer while I heavily slouch
All I've got left is a distant memory
Of a virile young lad that used to be me
Life is not good, it's totally rotten
For my youth has gone but not forgotten.

16) THE GHOST WRITER

Elaine Murdock sat staring at her laptop, the murder mystery story she was writing had come to a stop due to the writers nightmare, writers block. Having written thousands of words, many characters with twists and turns, things had been going well but now she had a problem. A coffee and rest away from the screen might help, she thought, but after twenty minutes, the body rested, the mind refused to do so and was constantly searching for the answers she so desired to finish her hopefully best seller, but they were not forthcoming.

With no children and husband Jeffrey at work, there was little to distract her but the ideas eluded her. After a quick phone call she switched off the laptop, tousled her hair and adorned some bright red lipstick. A short drive and she was greeted at the door of her lovers house. She stepped inside, they embraced and within minutes were naked enjoying passionate lovemaking on the floor of the hallway. He ferociously pushed himself inside her, she let out a deep cry, her well-manicured nails gouging into his muscular tanned torso. The lust and passion lasted for about fifteen minutes before she screamed, 'Yes, yes, oh yes' as he powered his body into hers, eventually coming to an out of control climax. They lay there side by side, hands together, soaking up the adrenaline now flowing through their bodies. Her mind became totally relaxed, all thoughts of plots, characters, ideas, now removed. 'I love you,' she whispered. He responded with a squeeze of her hand and gently leaned over her naked breasts; with a loving kiss he repeated her words. Over a coffee they chatted about how they should be together for the rest of their lives. Patrick her lover did not have a problem being single but Elaine's husband, Jeffrey would never give her a divorce or give up without a fight. There was also huge financial issues involved including property and insurance policies which would make Elaine a very rich woman should anything happen to her husband.

Over the next few weeks a plan was made to solve all their problems. Elaine and Jeffrey set sail on a pre booked cruise around the Mediterranean, not by chance, Patrick was also on the cruise. After about a week in the middle of the sea, they began to put their plan into action. One evening, Jeffrey was taking in the atmosphere of the beautiful moonlit night as he strolled along the deck. He stopped and looked up at the millions of stars and thought how lucky he was to have such a wonderful wife and way of life. His magical moment was short lived as he stood in a dark area and saw his wife having sex with her lover under the stairs. The shock was immense, he froze, unable to look away, eventually he wandered off in the opposite direction, falling in a heap onto a sunbed. His mind was awash with mixed emotions, anger and rage, plus the nagging question, why! He hit the bars, becoming blind drunk with a bottle of whiskey in hand. He failed to return to his cabin that night, a full search of the ship was made but he was never found. Patrick, Elaine's lover, took the opportunity to uphold his part of the plan and told her he had pushed Jeffrey overboard, hundreds of miles from land. 'Now we can be together' he said. Elaine thought through the circumstances, no more living a lie in a miserable marriage plus, with the wealth she could do as she pleased, no witnesses to a perfect murder, well one, Patrick. Two days later, Patrick disappeared, presumed to have fallen overboard.

A week later, the cruise over, Elaine returned home. The following day she fell into the arms of her true love, the young, handsome and virile cousin of Patrick. 'We will have to do that again sometime,' he said. After returning home from a night of passion with her toy boy, she switched on her laptop to add new ideas to her story. She read the last chapter again and again. Her faced drained as she knew she had not written it. 'My computer has been hacked,' she thought. Two nights later another chapter appeared, it was compelling, brilliantly written, full of mystery, far better than any of her ideas. In a desperate bid to become a best-selling writer, she told no one and became engrossed in the final chapters. At last it was finished; she had her best seller. A few nights later there was one final message. I hope you are happy with your book; I have e-mailed the insurance companies and changed the name of the beneficiary in my will. Have a nice life, the Police are on the way, your ever thoughtful ghost writer, Jeffrey.

17) THE CHAMPION

Was I having an anxiety attack or were my nerves just playing up, either way this was not a good time. Must keep it under control but it was difficult in such stressful circumstances. I felt my heart pumping as I lay in pole position, a bead of sweat irritated my forehead, the palms of my hands were hot and sticky with an annoying itch. My chest became tight as I checked my pacemaker, all seemed fine, I just need to calm down. I glanced at the fearsome opposition, much younger than me with a powerful drive to be the best and win. Was this the cause of my anxiety, was I becoming inferior being older. Yes I thought, I have to prove myself, I have to win at all costs. The countdown began, I gripped the steering wheel, the bead of sweat fell on my nose causing slight distraction, the red light flashed to green, I accelerated and in my mind was the smell of rubber. The Ferrari powered off down the racetrack. A 100 mph in seconds as the first bend loomed up ahead, a change of gear and powerful thrust as the car gripped the track and sped round the bend. My hands were rigid on the steering wheel, my body feeling the strain. A great start as I left the bend and headed down the straight. I checked to see the opposition behind, powering after me. Being in the lead caused my anxiety levels to drop but there was a long way to go. Lap after lap I stayed ahead but only by seconds, one false mistake and it could all change. The atmosphere was electric as suddenly the second place car was alongside me, full throttle. I just had to hang on until the next bend, it was then that the Ferrari came into its own, the dynamics, the quality engineering and of course the driver.

Now neck and neck, the bend came up fast, one split second too soon or too late could decide the winner. A quick change of gear brake and acceleration in a second with perfect timing and the Ferrari flew round the bend causing the opposition to clip the chicane, spin off the track and hit the safety barrier upside down.

with the driver safe and the emergency services dealing with the smouldering wreck, I gave a burst and was over the line. I felt excited but the strain and tension had eased, I had won, I had done it, I was the champion. My opposition burst into tears, he so wanted to win. As he stormed off he shouted, 'Dad, it's just a game, it's not real, it's scale electrix.

That's Rich

18) HOLIDAY BLUES

I shuddered as the sleet and rain beat against the windows in sub-zero temperature. I stood there fully clothed with my super warm 'onesie' over the top, staring out at the utter bleak miserable day. The electric heater, although two kilowatts, was in a bewildered world as it desperately tried to put some warmth into the cold room. Ice had formed on the inside of the windows and heavy condensation was beginning to blur my view. The central heating engineer said he would be here as soon as possible but he was inundated with calls for help.

I curled up on the settee with the cat who seemed totally oblivious to my plight and did not appear to have a care in the world apart from me disturbing it from a deep slumber. I felt the warmth of its body as I softly stroked it and cuddled up close while it purred away totally contented. Suddenly the heater gave a groan as its glowing bars slowly diminished to a cold grey much to the discomfort of the cat. I moved and pressed the light switch, nothing, the electric was off. The temperature plummeted as my 'onesie' fought to retain the heat. My feet lay inside thick socks with the 'onesie' over them in an attempt to keep the cold at bay. After an hour or so my face began to hurt, my nose was reduced to a constant sniff, keeping in tune with the cats purring. I flicked through a magazine hoping it would take my mind off things.

It was mid-February, an advertisement for a luxury cruise to Barbados caught my eye. If only, I thought as my mind began to wander. I found some old travel brochures and over the next hour I convinced myself I needed an exotic holiday even though I was out of work, on benefits and struggling to pay my bills. I got changed and headed for the local travel agents where I got completely lost in exotic destinations around the world. I took a few brochures and headed home. The electric was back on, the heating engineer arrived to tell me I needed a new boiler. That did it, enough is enough, I was going on holiday.

Over the following week I trawled through the brochures hoping to find an exotic holiday package that would fit in with the remaining credit on my card. I returned to the travel agents and sat in a quiet corner by the heated radiator, my mind awash with fabulous thoughts.

Eventually I sat on the plane feeling excited as I headed out to Barbados.

Lying on the golden beach, swimming in fabulous clear blue waters surrounded by palm trees with mountains stretching far and wide. Not a cloud in the sky and so warm. My house with its broken boiler was becoming lost at the back of my mind.

After my arrival, I was sitting at the beach bar watching the ripples of the sea when a gorgeous tanned hunk of a man bought me a cocktail, showered me with compliments, took me for a swim and eventually back to his luxury villa where we spent the night together making love. The following morning he asked me if I would like to move in with him. I was just about to say 'yes' when there was a tap on my shoulder. I opened my eyes, there in front of me was the sea, a golden beach, palm trees and mountains and a beach bar, totally an exotic scene. 'I'm sorry to disturb you miss but we are closing in five minutes.' My dreams shattered, I left the travel agents with its fabulous pictures on the walls and headed home clutching more brochures.

19) COUGHIN' UP.

The bailiff's letter was no surprise

A week to pay! lay before my eyes

The rents immoral, far too high

This is my home, I began to cry

I cannot work, a broken leg

I sent a reply, a desperate beg

On deaf ears my words did lay

The landlord replied, 'nothin' to say'

A week went by, a knock at the door

You pay now or it will cost you more

I've got no work, I've got no money

They looked at my leg, thought it funny

A restraining order in my hand

Pay up now!, only seven grand

We'll take your goods, telly and pet

If our demands are not met

They arrived one day, took all I had

In total despair, I was really sad

My new home was dark, small and had nothin'

But do you really need much, in a coffin!

20) WELL BLOW ME

'If your drunk when you come in then sleep in the back room, I'm fed up with you waking me up and clawing your hands all over me,' said Andy's wife Mary.

He set off on a pub crawl with his mate Tom. Six pubs and a few hours later, they ended up in Yates Wine Lodge a bit worse for wear. Ladies of the night gathered round for free drinks then smooched and swayed on the dance floor, one barely able to keep Andy on his feet. Much later Andy staggered out into a dark alleyway and eventually collapsed on the floor outside a sleazy sex shop.

He arrived home in a taxi and fell through the doorway, landing at his wife's feet. 'Your disgusting and you stink of perfume. As he crawled to the settee, she saw the lipstick on his shirt. 'You've had sex with another woman,' she yelled, 'I've had enough, I want a divorce.' He denied everything and curled up on the settee.

The next morning there was a knock at the door, on opening it she found a taxi driver standing there. 'I think your husband left this in my cab' She took the item and closed the door. She sat there not knowing whether to laugh or cry as she stared at the item while her husband snored away. After hiding it under the bed, she set off for work.

The following night after midnight, he quietly opened her bedroom door, the bedside lamp was on clearly showing his wife cuddled up to another woman. He was shocked but aroused at the same time. With adrenalin pumping, he stared for a few moments then gently closed the door and went back to bed.

After work the following day he went to his local pub, his mind had been in turmoil all day and he had no idea how he was going to handle the situation. A bloke in her bed was one thing, a quick punch in the face would sort that, but a woman, he was lost, bewildered and angry. He supped his pint, then another and another, eventually his mind descending into a nightmare world.

His mate Tom came in and he poured his woes onto him, how his life was being destroyed. A few more mates gathered round to listen to his tale, intrigued and stimulated at the thought of his wife with another woman. They taunted him with wisecracks, he began to sink lower into depression. Just then his wife walked in with her new bed partner and pushed her into her husband's arms. His mates fell about in hysterics and took pictures on their mobiles as Andy fell forward, his face now deeply embedded into the large breasts of the sexy blow up doll he had nicked from outside the sex shop the other night.

That's Rich

21) A WORLD AT WAR

What is the future, what lies ahead?
When do we stop burying our dead?
Sons and daughters in the forces
Orphaned children, life changing courses
Always at war in a foreign land
A fight to the death over a stretch of sand
Internal issues should not be our fight
But look at the people, look at their plight
Blown to bits by a government force
Seeking out rebels fighting their cause
Fighting for towns, no peace in sight
As bombing continues throughout the night
Millions displaced from their homeland
As they trudge for miles over hot desert sand
Refugee camps, poverty galore
As countries say we can take no more
Hospitals, schools, flattened to a pile of rubble
Used by people who gave no trouble
In the cause of world power, is that why we fight
Not for the people, not for their plight
Is it for democracy on foreign soil?
Or is it the fact they've got lots of oil.

22) WHAT'S IN THE BOX

The death threats were taken very seriously, these were dangerous times, attacks on people were common and could strike at any time. Things had escalated in recent months and the young couple had to make a life changing decision. Should they stay in their hometown and risk injury or even death or move away from the area and try to start a new life in a hopefully more peaceful town.

Joe was a self-employed tradesman and could usually find enough work to look after him and his wife but their desire to have a family had added pressure on him as she was due to give birth soon. Eventually after two more innocent people had been murdered one night, they decided to move. With no transport of their own and not able to travel first class, they opted to hire an economy version. With their belongings packed, they set off on the long journey to a better life. They soon came across others who had taken the same decision and they banded together for safety. Their numbers grew, some armed as they entered a desert area known for attacks by bandit groups. The going was slow on the sandy track in the intense heat with no cover except for headscarves. At night the temperature dropped to near freezing as they huddled together round a fire, burning anything they could find. After clearing the desert they came across a river with welcome shade, fruits and vegetation. They followed its flow and after about a week they reached their destination. The town was busy, mostly refugees from other towns fleeing the dangers. They parked their transport and searched around for somewhere to stay, there was none. Others were lying outside in shaded areas but due to his wife's condition Joe had to find somewhere under cover. Eventually room was found, the owner removed his transport and parked it outside. The smell was a bit obnoxious but at least it was warm and dry. The following day his wife began to give birth, a woman helper was on hand but the baby's arm got stuck and twisted, resulting in his wife's sheer pain. The woman could not free it. She looked up at Joe who was sat on a box looking very anxious. 'What's in the box', she screamed. 'My tools', he replied. She frantically searched the box and removed two smooth wooden prongs which she inserted and freed the baby's arm, allowing birth. The place erupted with cries of joy and happiness. 'Good job you had your toolbox with you Joe', said the woman. 'Yes, very fortunate', said the angel Gabriel.

That's Rich

23) SHATTERED DREAMS

Life, love and laughter were the topics of the day

As we sauntered into school with lots of things to say

It was my birthday and I was so excited

Along with my friends who were all delighted

Life was so exciting as we looked to the future

Then settled down to study with our classroom tutor

The silence was amazing as brains began to grind

In search of the answers their project was to find

The silence was suddenly shattered as this scene fell apart

And my best friend Angie was shot through the heart

He had burst through the door with evil in his head

And in a matter of minutes all my friends were dead

Blood was all around me, the screams chilling and loud

As I fell to the floor, my head quickly bowed

The gunfire was deafening with death all around

I lay there injured on the bloodied ground

Silence then returned apart from heavy moans and groans

From mutilated friends with bullets in their bones

Families destroyed, the grief too much to bare

But do government officials ever really care

No control of guns held by the masses

And more and more shootings in U.S school classes.

24) FAMILY BUSINESS

Mary Johnson was raised by her aunt, Billie Jean Moon, in Dallas Texas, as a result of her parents being killed in a car crash when she was six years old. She later graduated and qualified as a nurse and worked in the local hospital. She married quite young and some years later, she and her husband Grant moved to New South Wales in Australia where she had secured a job as a paediatrician.

As the years passed by, Grant who was a lot older than her, became terminally ill and Mary had to give up her job to look after him. It was a physically tiring task coupled with the mental strain of watching the person you love, slowly die. Even though she was a nurse, she had to find inner strength to cope, eventually Grant passed away. She was devastated but somewhat relieved as his pain and suffering was no more and her stress and strain gradually eased after a period of mourning.

Grant had been a special forces marine in the British army and had been decorated and presented with a letter of commendation from the Royal family for his services as a security Commander. Mary was very proud of this and sent it to her aunt who she was very close to. Grants death changed Mary's thoughts on life, having cared for him she decided that it would be nice to care for other mature, terminally ill, people. As a result, she changed her job and became a senior care nurse.

She was in regular touch with her aunt, but as time passed she too became old and frail. Mary had no choice, she had to go back. This woman had given her so much love and affection, it was only fair and morally right that she went to look after her in her final years. She said her goodbyes in Australia and returned to Dallas.

She barely recognized the vivacious, always smiling woman she left behind all those years ago, even though she was now ninety years old, life had not been kind to her. She was bedridden and unable to do much for herself. Mary moved back into her old room, almost untouched since she left, childhood possessions still lay on the dressing table.

Looking after her aunt was no easy task but she now had years of experience which she was thankful for. Daily meals, dressing and washing her, shopping, sorting out her personal requirements, banking, bills, were all part of the daily chores.

One day some time later, her aunt, now barely able to move, asked Mary to get some things out of the dressing table drawers. This was no ordinary dressing table, built by her brother-in-law many years ago out of solid oak from a tree that was struck by lightning in his back garden. It was like a fortress. All the years Mary lived there, never ever had she seen inside it, the key was always kept in a secret place. She had childhood dreams of what lay inside and used to make up fantasy stories about the contents. Mary asked for the whereabouts of the key and her aunt pointed to an old wooden box containing puzzles which she had kept since she was a child. Mary was well aware of the box and had on occasions opened it to find puzzles, bits of jewellery and an old, faded ticket to a show on Broadway. Her aunt explained that her sister and partner took her as a special birthday treat to see the show and spend a few days in New York.

Mary passed the box to her aunt who's eye sight was now failing. She put on her glasses and Mary watched in amazement as frail wrinkled fingers slowly removed the base inside to reveal an old solid brass key. She passed it to Mary who was now feeling very excited at the thought of opening the dressing table and revealing its contents which had kept her intrigued all these years. She slowly inserted the key, opened the top draw and removed various items which she placed on the bed. Her aunt showed her the items and explained what they were. She held an old leather wallet, 'this had belonged to my sister's partner and this now out of date booklet driving licence was also his'. Mary did not recognize the name.

Her aunt held a photograph of two babies, 'twins' she said, 'I had a romantic affair with a handsome soldier while your uncle was away in the army for a few years, I had them adopted, he found out and that's why we got divorced, no one else alive knows'.

She asked Mary to open the next drawer and take out the contents, a shiver went through her as there lay a rifle and a shotgun in gleaming condition. 'They're not loaded are they aunty'. 'No, they are very old, put them here'. Mary carefully laid them on the bed. 'Pass me the woolly hat as well'. She took out a navy blue hand knitted hat which had a hole through the top of it. Mary sat on the bed, now in total awe of what lay before her. Her aunt was quite distressed as she took a couple of deep breathes and began her story.

'This one is a Remington self-loading shotgun and the other is a very powerful Browning automatic rifle, they were both used by my sister and partner, the hat had a bullet fired through it which killed my sister.

'Everything here now belongs to you'.
Before I got married to your uncle and became
Mrs Moon, my name was Billie Jean Parker and

my sister who you will not remember, was Bonnie Parker who was married to Clyde Chestnut Barrow, they were otherwise known as the notorious 'Bonnie and Clyde'. Mary stood there speechless just as her aunt took her last breath and passed away.

That's Rich

82

25) LOOK UP TO THE STARS

One night I stood outside my house and looked up to the stars

Way on past the moon I looked for Jupiter and Mars

With a billion twinkling lights, which way could they be

But a cloud passed by and soon no longer could I see

To the left, to the right, oh so many I'll be here all night

Suddenly a bright twinkle caught the centre of my eye

I can see Mars, I can see Mars, I began to cry

I peered down at my feet to accustom to the night

When I looked up to the stars again, I saw a wonderful sight

There was the magical Jupiter with many a glorious ring

So far and distant but I could hear someone sing

'Fly me to the moon and let me play among the stars

Let me see what spring is like on Jupiter and Mars'

I focussed my telescope and saw a rocket departin'

And waving from a window was the smiling face of The legendary Dean Martin.

26) FIVE MINUTE WARNING

'This is Dave Anderson with the B.B.C six o'clock news.

'The ongoing tensions between the United States of America and North Korea have virtually reached a point of no return with the U.S ready to strike and remove the looming threat of nuclear war with the communist country.

'The American naval fleet, the most powerful in the world, now has its three main nuclear aircraft carriers, together with cruisers and destroyers, plus more than a hundred F16 and F35 fighter planes on full alert and in striking range of the North Korean capital. For the latest update we pass you over to Andy Simms, our world affairs correspondent who is in the South Korean capital, Seoul.

'Andy, could you give us the latest news on the tense situation there.'

Reporter: 'Well the word tense is probably a mild description considering the state of play. The U.S has reached the end of the road, any talks on the situation have been rebuffed by the dictator Kim Jung-Un who seems to think the only outcome is all out war, not just any war but a full blown nuclear war.'

Newsreader: 'But he knows his missiles cannot yet reach the U.S coastline, so what is the point?'

Reporter: 'His threats extend to South Korea, mainly the capital where the Americans have anti-missile equipment including the all-powerful THAAD which is now fully operational. He has also threatened to destroy the aircraft carriers plus the Japanese convoy which is assisting the U.S in exercises.'

Newsreader: 'Most of his recent rocket trials have been a failure, so what makes him think he will be successful, surely it's a bluff.'

Reporter: 'Bluff or not, it's one the Americans are not going to take any chances on, it will only be a matter of time before the rogue state acquires the knowledge to build rockets capable of reaching the U.S and the American government will not allow that to happen.'

Newsreader: 'What is the Russian and Chinese response to this dangerous situation.?'

Reporter: 'Neither are happy about it, they have both tried talks and sanctions. China supplies them with oil but seems unwilling to cut it off altogether as they are their only ally. Russia is not happy as they border the rogue state and are concerned they will be exposed to the western world should an attack take place but they have made it known they will not intervene unless directly threatened and the same applies to China.'

Newsreader: 'If an attack occurs, when is it likely to be?'

Reporter: 'I am afraid the word "If" is no longer in the equation. "When" could be anytime, today, tomorrow, next week, who knows, there is one thing for certain, the world will never be the same again.'

Newsreader: 'What are the feelings of residents in Seoul who are in constant daily threat of their lives.'

Reporter: 'A high percentage are grateful the Americans are there but others think they have escalated the problem and would like them to withdraw.'

Reporter: 'Oh my God, oh my God, missiles are flying overhead.'

Newsreader: 'Which way Andy, which way?'

Reporter: 'Towards North Korea from the South, high up, it's started, the war has started. Oh my God, more missiles, loud explosions, we can only presume they are intercepting North Korean rockets. People are running everywhere, trying to shelter, screaming in fear.'

Newscaster: 'Can you see any North Korean rockets Andy; can you see any?' A minute later there was a massive explosion.

Newsreader: 'Andy, Andy!'

27) MOTORING MEMORIES

We need a new one I said to my wife
We've had this for years, we deserve better in life
Well you're the driver so I don't mind
Any ideas of make, model, what kind

Something sporty in silver and black
With whitewall tyres front and back
Leather trim, walnut dash
Sounds expensive, have we got the cash

Endowment policy due up next week
With a rise in pension and a financial tweak
We can buy something new, totally class
With a removable soft top and tinted glass

So into the showroom they boldly went
And were met by a salesman, a dapper gent
We would like a new model and we'll pay cash
It's got to go fast and look really flash
It's your lucky day, cried the dapper gent
As off down the road they quickly went
I'll put my foot down, blast the hooter
Oh, I'm so excited with our new mobility scooter.

28) THINGS IN GENERAL

Two and a half pounds I weighed, the day that I was born

My lungs where so small and I lay there all forlorn

Would I live, would I die, to the nurses my mother did cry

Save my baby! save my baby! the words they did fly

They saved her baby, they saved my life

But as I grew, there was trouble and strife

I became a bouncer and a minder to the stars

I kept them safe and escorted them to their cars

Tom Jones, Debbie Harry and many others

I protected and cared for them, just like their mothers

But as time passed, things changed and I began to run a pub

With my lovely wife Rose, we served fine ale and first class grub

At six foot one and shoulders wide

Into bad habits I did slide

Drinking, smoking and late, late nights

Managing the pub, sorting out fights

And over the years my health did decline

From the effects of birth, smoking, beer and wine
Now my lungs are not efficient
As the amount of air is insufficient
A nebuliser I have to puff
And life has become pretty rough
Two strokes I've had and nearly died
As Rose my wife sat by my side
One more could kill you said the doc
So don't be jogging round the block
Blood pressure high, lungs not good
As the results came back from my blood
But then last week I had a bad turn
And from the doctor I was soon to learn
Sixteen to nineteen hours I had left to live
As my body shut down, I had nothing to give
Rushed to the hospital by Richard and Linda
Put in a bed close to the winda'
Antibiotics, medicines galore
I was so weak; I could take no more
But the doctors and nurses were simply great
As very slowly they improved my heart rate
And a few days later as I lay in bed
Brought back to life, back from the dead

I laughed and joked with a sense of humour

Knowing I didn't have a life threatening tumour

But to laugh, joke, be funny, is it a sin

For it is something I never did before I went in.

Thank you all for your wonderful attention and care

And to all my friends, your praises I will share.

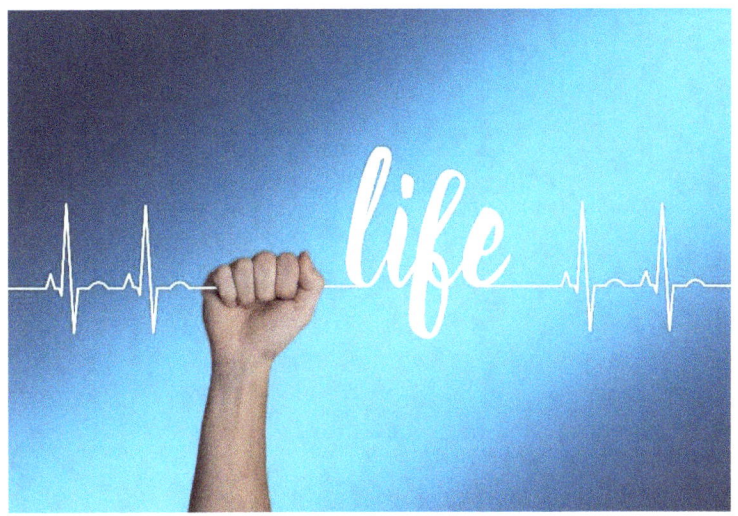

That's Rich

29) THE HOUSE BY THE SEA.

We bought a house by the sea

A little love nest for you and me

To watch the sunset was totally bliss

As we cuddled up close with a kiss

In the summer at the bottom of our plot

We'd lie on the grass amongst the daisies and forget-me-not

The tweeting birds and a butterfly

Enhancing the view from where we lie

A passing boat alone in the deep blue

We love our house with its wonderful view

It's right on the cliff, way up high

We can see for miles across sea and sky

But the foaming waves pounded the land

Eroding the cliffs, turning them to sand

And over the years our garden has crumbled

As the raging sea steadily rumbled

Now twenty years later it's up to the door

And our lovely garden is sadly no more

Nature has called and made its path

And there's no way we can stop its wrath

Our house will fall into the sea

Leaving us homeless, having to flee
No insurance or compensation
For having to stay with a relation
We loved our house with its view
The sea and sky ever so blue
But nature won and now it's in the sea
Leaving us with just a beautiful memory

30) DAZED AND CONFUSED

'Good morning Mr Chow, welcome to your first driving lesson, we are going to sit in the car and I will explain the controls,' said the driving instructor.

'I see,' replied Mr Chow.

'This is the gear lever.'

'I see.' 'This is first gear, very slow or up hill'

'I see.'

'Second gear a bit faster.'

'I see.' '

'Third gear usually in traffic.'

'I see.'

'Fourth gear for normal driving at a steady speed, forty to fifty miles per hour'

'I see.'

'Fifth gear for main roads, seventy miles per hour'

'I see.'

'Finally, sixth gear for cruising on motorways.'

'I see.'

'You don't speak much English Mr Chow.'

'No, I learning.'

'I see' said the instructor.

'Yes, I see,' replied Mr Chow.

'If you want to go backwards slowly, you use this gear, push it down and across.'

'I see'

'To put the car into gear you press the clutch down and go into first gear.'

'I see'

'This is the handbrake'

'I see.'

'Press the button on the end and let the handbrake down.'

'I see'

'Very slowly let your foot off the clutch.'

'I see'

'At the same time gently press on the pedal on the right, that is the accelerator.'

'I see'

'The pedal in the middle is the brake, it stops the car when you press it.'

'I see.' Mr Chow looked at the instructor with a confused expression and pointed at his legs, 'one, two, I no have three.'

'I see,' said the instructor, I will show you.' Over the next hour they went through the control motions. 'That is what you have to learn.'

'I see,' said Mr Chow. Over the next few weeks he began to improve even though they had not yet left the instructors private car park.

'Next week we will go on the road, a quiet one.'

'I see.'

The time came and the instructor drove to a quiet road. 'You can drive from here.'

'I see.' Chow nervously sat in the drivers' seat and moved off. First gear, second gear, third gear with a shudder. He soon became a more competent and positive driver and one afternoon whilst driving through the countryside he approached a bend a bit too fast.

'Slow down,' said the instructor, but it was too late.

The car spun out of control off the bend, crashed through a wooden fence into a field and hit a large oak tree. The instructor was killed instantly. Chow woke up injured in hospital two days later.

The Police came to interview him and take a statement. 'This is a serious matter, the instructor is dead,' the officer told him. 'What was the cause of the accident Mr Chow.

'I tell him, I tell him, I tell him all the time, the road is icy, icy, icy, he no listen.'

31) YOU ARE ALWAYS ON MY MIND

No benefits for me so I'm out on the street

Just a scrounger they said, get back on your feet

They reckon I was fit for work but they haven't got a clue

Who would give me a job if they really knew?

Sort yourself out, get a wash and a shave

Common remarks daily, with two fingers I wave

A new suit and tie, a different person you would be

But you can't cover up what's wrong with me

You can't see my problem, it hides deep inside my brain

And each and every day it drives me insane

The world is just a fantasy, a total lost cause

It's like being an adult who believes in Santa Claus

The different of right and wrong is scrambled in my head

And often in my life I wish that I was dead

I do need a job and some wealth

But that's not going to happen until they sort out my mental health.

Before you moan about the rain outside your window ....count your blessings.

32) I FELT SICK

Five years I had been in my home, it was nothing special, but it was mine. A bit more space would have been nice but I managed. My bed was a bit basic, typical cheap wood, no headboard and there was a draft through the roof at times. I used to go up there and inspect it but it was so full of gaps little could be done apart from a temporary cover. It was much the same with the front door, the lock was always jamming on the outside so I stayed in most days.

The toilet reminded me of my grandparents, a piece of wood with your bum over the side, not very hygienic and I felt sick at times as the smell was awful. Cleaning it was not a nice job but it had to be done, otherwise I would have suffocated. The so called bathroom was not very desirable as there was no bath or shower, just a bowl of water to splash my face and sprinkle my unmentionables.

As for the kitchen, it's a good job I am not a Gordon Ramsey tribute, it was so basic, plus I can't cook, although I do tend to swear a lot. Nowadays I eat much the same thing.

Eventually due to a shared ownership scheme, I was transferred to a larger home with a good solid roof and spacious interior. There was a separate bathroom and the loo, although basic, was at the rear. The front door worked perfect and I was able to come and go as I pleased, often spending hours outside on the veranda.

One day an old friend came to visit me, we used to meet up at the local garden centre many years ago. I gave him something to eat and drink and we had a long chat and I mean long as he suffered from a bad stutter and kept repeating himself. He told me that life had not been good, he had been very ill due to malnutrition caused by lack of care at an overcrowded home. As a result he became very weak and realised that if he didn't leave, he would die.

Being a big softie and having lots of room, I told him he was welcome to stay with me for a while until he got better. Several weeks later I was becoming demented as he kept moaning about everything.

'I-I I'm c-c-c cold, cold a-a-a and it's d-d-d dark in here.

It's 2.00.am, you have got a bed and a feather quilt, now get to sleep.'

'I-I c-c-c can't, the beds h-h-h hard and I feel s-s-s sick.

He felt sick, I felt sick as I opened the door and said, 'On yer bike, on yer bike, on yer bike.' Why do you k-k-k keep repeating yourself,' he asked.

I replied, 'Cos I'm a bloody parrot you moron.'

That's Rich

33) GRIEF AND ANXIETY

It's been six long years since I lost my son
No longer here to hug his mum
He went out one night with his mate
But never again came through our gate

A peaceful lad, wouldn't hurt a fly
So why on that night did he have to die
Someone tell me, someone explain
He will never be back but it may ease my pain

Why did he die on that fateful night?
I need to know, it is my right
The Mayor of London, Sadia Khan
Says that he's doing the best that he can

He's put in plans for preventive controls
But try telling that to all the dead souls
A waste of life and grief for kin
Due to the colour of their skin

A lack of Police and law and order
Just more work for the Coroners recorder
Is anyone bothered, does anyone care
Just another statistic on Facebook to share

So how do we stop this loss of life
Apart from shooting every thug carrying a knife.

34) THE PARANORMAL

John Goodwin had a very disturbed adolescent life. His abnormal interest in the paranormal, ghosts, spooks, fairies, was of great concern not only to himself but his parents and close family and friends. He had searched his mind many times to find an answer to his strange behaviour but none was forthcoming. Close mates began to slowly drift away, unable to deal with his strange mind. Where it had come from, where it was going, he had no idea.

Years later, now married to Karen; he was even more engrossed in the subject but due to his wife having a similar state of mind he was able to keep things under control. They had met at a meeting of the paranormal society where like members expressed their views and released their inner thoughts. Their neighbours and very close friends, Anita and Peter, shared their beliefs as they too were members of the society and they would often meet up to release their feelings and share a few drinks. Over the years they became very close, maybe a bit too close but nothing was ever suggested that they were anything else than best friends. Karen socialised with Anita a lot and they were almost inseparable, like sisters. John and Peter also had a close bond enjoying many hours on the golf course.

As time passed, John began to find Karen's attitude towards him becoming rather distant, resulting in a lack of interest in their married life. He became concerned that she was having an affair, but if true, who with.

Several months later, Peter received the dreadful news that Anita had been killed in a car crash. Naturally he was devastated but the support he received from his close friends was most welcome. Anita was buried in the local cemetery, she never believed in crematoriums, that was too final, there was always an afterlife as far as she was concerned. Karen became moody and depressed at the loss of her friend and after a short while she told John she would be going to the local bingo two or three times a week to take her mind off things. John welcomed her intentions as the atmosphere in the house was becoming a strain. As time passed, Karen's moods towards John became increasingly uncomfortable and his mind once again wandered, making him believe she was having an affair. On her trips to the bingo, he began to follow her but for some unknown reason she always managed to disappear into thin air. One evening, having given up following her, he decided on the way back to pay a visit to Anita's grave. He knelt down and verbally began to pour his heart out to her even though she no longer existed. He told her of his passionate love for her and how he missed their torrid love making on secret meetings. 'Anita, Anita, screamed Karen as she lay embraced and naked against her, 'It's John, It's John, he's pouring out his dying love for you.' It was then that Karen realised that her best friend and lover had been having an affair with her husband. 'You bitch, you bitch,' she screamed as she began to ascend from the grave and shuddered as her spirit passed by John who was totally oblivious to the events going on around him. He continued to let Anita know of his feelings as Karen hovered nearby. On return home, John was surprised to find Karen naked in bed in a very amorous mood. She came to the conclusion that if John could have so much love and passion for another, it should be with her, at least that way Anita's death will not have been in vain. 'I love you John, she whispered as she snuggled up. John gave a contented sigh of relief, happy that he had got the love of his wife back and his torrid affair with Anita would never be known by anyone.

35) THE WALK OF LIFE

You have got to be desperate to abandon your life

Leave your homeland with kids and wife

Escape from violence, poverty and despair

In the hope of a future in a land out there

It drives us on, it creates desire

Stirs our minds, fills our hearts with fire

From central America across rivers and land

From Guatemala, El Salvador, Honduras, places not grand

Our numbers swell as we cover each mile

By people desperate for a life with a smile

A thousand miles they trudge on foot

With a lack of food and an aching gut

Totally focussed on their destination

They suffer thirst and mild infestation

Now in their thousands, a problem for Trump

As the caravan of people steadily clump

The Mexican border lies up ahead
The gateway to freedom or a bullet in the head
For their path is blocked into the States
By border control and iron gates

'Send in the troops,' cries Trump in dismay
Get rid of these criminals before election day.

36) ARE YOU LISTENING

Hi, how are you today

Sorry I'm late, met a friend on the way

Someone from school, many years ago

Couldn't remember her name, but no one you would know

I have brought you some flowers to brighten up your home

Plus some plastic fencing and a little garden gnome

I'll take out the weeds before I go

Clean up the front, give you a glow

Next door is looking a little rough

But being elderly, it must be tough

No friends or family ever come near

As time passes by year after year

Cold and damp, rain and snow

But they've got nowhere else they can go

I'll spend some time, help them out

It's a lot of work, I have no doubt

What do you think, should I help another?

Are you listening to me from your grave, mother?

37) ELF & SAFETY

A week before Christmas Johns wife Mary walked into their laminate floored lounge and slipped on the pool left by the dog, breaking two bones in her arm. As a result she was kept in hospital for a few days. She told John that the dog had to go as it was consistently peeing, smelling and a danger to others. John was not very handy around the house but as a result of her predicament, Mary asked John if he would put the Christmas tree up along with the decorations. He set about the task and a couple of hours later the room was transformed into a festive theme. John stood back and admired his work, the lights were flashing, reflecting on the tinsel and coloured balls. Gold stars shone brightly as angels glistened and reindeer and their sleigh glowed as Father Christmas sat with lots of presents. A few sprays of snow from a can over the pine leaves completed the scene apart from the elves and the most important one of all, the fairy queen. He reached deep into the box and spread the elves around the tree followed by the fairy for which he had to stand on a stool to give her pride of place at the very top. John felt proud as he straightened her bent pink wand, task completed.

John decided that he deserved a treat for his efforts and set off for the pub. As he got to the garden gate he turned round to look at his handiwork shining brightly through the bay window. Again he felt proud as a passing neighbour gave a pleasing remark.

That night as John lay sleeping and his lights twinkled away, things began to happen. The elves became restless, but one particular elf was being badly affected by the flashing lights causing him to malfunction in a rogue manner. He began to climb up towards the fairy queen, eventually grabbing at her dress. After several attempts the fairy was somewhat annoyed and waved her magic wand but it bent on a branch and fell to the floor. Another tug of her dress and she kicked the elf away. The following day John found the broken wand and went to the fairy shop and bought another one.

That night the rogue elf kicked off again with the lights affecting his mind. He climbed up to the fairy and began pulling her dress time and time again. The fairy was becoming distraught but suddenly the cat jumped up at the tree attempting to grab a chocolate bar. The tree fell, the cat landed on the floor, the elf fell onto the back of the cat, the cat freaked out and began to run round the room, leaping across the furniture while the elf clung onto the cats collar, legs trailing in mid-air, fearing for its life. Just then, the family

Rottweiler poked its head in the doorway, barking constantly, wondering what was going on. The cat, fearsome of the dog, dug its claws into the rug which slid across the room, hit the coffee table and came to a dead stop. The elf went head over heels as it flew through the air just as the fairy waved her magic wand. In a split second, the elf was turned into a snowball, it hit the door with force and slid to the floor, melting into a pool of water. Just then, John, who had been sound asleep, walked into the room to see what all the commotion was about. He slipped on the pool of water, broke his arm in two places and murmured, 'that dog has got to go.'

An hour later he lay on a hospital bed, Mary

turned to him and said, 'how did you get on with the Christmas tree.' John replied, 'oh fine, just a slight problem with elf and safety.

That's Rich

38) IN THE EYES OF A CHILD

Six years old, what has she done
Apart from living, having fun
Playing with her loving sister
And the neighbour's boy who once kissed her
Childhood dreams, a fantasy land
A whole life ahead, looking grand
Mum and Dad working hard all day
While she's at school, then out to play
With her best friend and other mates
She never strays far from the gates
And at six o'clock every night
Her parents arrive to her delight
Daddy's her favourite as she gives him a hug
Makes his tea in his favourite mug
'I love you Daddy, you're the best'
'Enjoy your tea, have a rest'
Then one day as she stood by the gate
She realised daddy was very late
A phone call to mummy who's face went white
To say that daddy was arrested last night
'What is it mummy, what is wrong'
'Sit down dear this may take long'

'There's been a bit of a situation'

'Daddy's been arrested by immigration'

'Will he be home later tonight?'

Mummy looked at her daughter's plight

'No he won't,' she said with a sigh

And the childs tears ran as she began to cry

'He has not got identification'

'To coincide with new legislation'

'They're talking about segregation'

'Due to a political violation'

'There's lots of protests and condemnation'

'And it could mean permanent separation'

'Way beyond our imagination'

'Human rights,' screamed the little girl

Who's head was now in a total whirl

The United Nations she came to conclusion

But the mother knew she was in delusion

They're making out a social order

'To send him back to the Mexican border'

'It's re-direction to a place of correction'

'Does that mean tomorrow; I'll get no affection'

'Not now, not then, maybe never'

'These Politicians think they are so clever'

'Destroying the life of an innocent child'
'Who loves her daddy so meek and mild'
'No love, no touch. No big hug'
As she lies by the fire on a soft rug
'Mummy! surely this law could be aborted'
'Bring back my Daddy, get Trump deported'

That's Rich

39) OPERATION MARKET GARDEN

To capture nine bridges was the aim
'Operation Market Garden' was the name
Ten thousand soldiers bravely fought
But eight thousand died or were caught.

We liberated Eindhoven and Nijmegen
With airborne forces, tanks and men
Over Netherlands all seemed fine
Until we came to the River Rhine.

Enemy forces had gathered strong
Somehow the plans had all gone wrong
Mistakes were made by the top brass
And now the enemy has whipped our ass.

The battles lost, what should I do
I'll write a letter just for you
I'm lying here with my mates who have died
Their bodies strewn by my side.

I cannot move, my legs are shot
And very soon they will start to rot
Then I'll join my mates who have died
But I'd rather be by your side.

The battles lost, what should I do
Shout out loud, 'I love you'
But don't wait for me, my bodies shot
These last few words is all I've got.

I fought for freedom and our son
And I hope one day when this war is done
People will remember my mates and me
Who sadly died but set them free?

40 WHAT I DIDN'T DO on HOLIDAY

I didn't watch Corrie Street, the nation's favourite soap.

I just lay on a sunbed with a G & T and for a tan I did hope

I didn't watch Emmerdale and visit the Woolpack pub

I sat by the sea with another G & T, waiting for my grub

I didn't watch the dreary news and all the Brexit farce

I sipped another G & T, turned over and tried to tan my arse

I didn't listen to Teresa May or the antics of Larry the cat

I just sipped another G & T and adjusted my large sunhat

I didn't tweet on Twitter, Facebook or What's App

I just lay on my sunbed and enjoyed a restful nap

I didn't watch homeless people begging in the street

I just sipped another G & T and rested my weary feet

I didn't go to work or suffer Monday morning

blues

I just sipped another G & T without a thought of shoes

I didn't sit in traffic or wait for a very late bus

I just sipped another G & T and never made a fuss

I didn't listen to the forecast of rain, hail and sleet

I had my eighth G & T, just a little treat

I lay beneath the parasol, trying to keep cool

Watching all the people frolicking in the pool

I didn't feel the pain as off my sunbed I fell

Eyes blurred, speech slurred, I wasn't very well

So next time I go on holiday, I'll bin the G & T's

For now I'm lying in hospital with two fractured bloody knees.

41) THE VETERAN'S PLIGHT

Join the Army read the governments blurb
Seek adventure and tour the world
But all this seemed totally absurd
As the true details were unfurled

Snowflakes and phone zombies is for what we plead
So why don't you apply
Your country wants you in desperate need
So step forward, don't be shy

Exciting adventure, sports and fun
Opportunities are there to be found
You may even get issued with a gun
When you step out on foreign ground

Healthcare and housing, a pension to admire
What more do you need in life?
But suddenly it's time to retire
And you realise you're in desperate strife

Young and maimed through fighting a war

A cause that's not your concern

Peace and democracy, greed for oil, what am I fighting for

As Politicians argue but don't really care, will they ever learn

Now a veteran, discharged and unfit

To the government I stake my claim

But I'm told there's no benefits from some halfwit

It appears it's my fault I am lame

So out on the streets, homeless and cold

As in a shop doorway I bed for the night

I tried my best to be brave and bold

But all they want now is for me to be out of sight.

42) THE INNOCENCE OF A CHILD

At four years old, Denzel is my bestest friend

We were born together in hospital, me at the front, him the other end

Our mums are close and our dads are mates

We live opposite each other with matching gates

We play out together, sometimes we sneak to the park

But we have to make sure we are home before dark

Other friends play with us but some make an excuse

I don't know why but they shout and give us abuse

Denzel gets scared so I hug him tight

He stands there shaking in total fright

Are they jealous because we are best mates?

Who live opposite each other with matching gates?

We are just two friends who play and have fun

From early morning to the setting sun

One day I called across the road but Denzel did not reply

He has gone missing, said his mum as I began to cry

We searched the neighbourhood but he was nowhere to be found

 We called out his name but there was nothing, not a sound

Off to the Police station to report him lost

He must be found soon at any cost

The Sergeant said can you describe him to me

I said, 'he is four years old and looks just like me.

43) BREXIT FARCE

What a mess this Brexit farce

Politicians, they're all my arse

In or out, leave or stay

They're a waste of space, not worth the pay

They never listen to the masses

Or ride on a bus with their passes

They're chauffer driven in a big flash car

Even though they don't go far

Expenses for that, fees for this

Surely they're all taking the piss

But things are changing, they're being booted out

And very soon they will have nowt

For Larry the cat now has the controls

And there's no room in here for a bunch of arseholes

That's Rich

44) PEACE AND TRANQUILLITY

There was pure silence as I woke and lay in bed on my back soaking up the peace and tranquillity as the morning rays of warm sunshine created shadows on the white walls as they fought their way through the foliage of the eucalyptus trees. I smiled knowing it was going to be another hot balmy day of serenity. I could feel the flow of calmness oozing through my body as I drifted off into my own little paradise.

The tingling on the back of my hand hanging out towards the floor was a pleasant sensation despite the fact it interrupted my moments of dreams and fantasy. I moved it below the duvet to resume my pleasure but it was short lived, soft paws could be felt moving across my body before a coarse tongue licked my face, causing my brain to react. I swept the cat away but it was persistent and by now totally irritating. 'Sod off,' I shouted, but it did not appear to understand. Eventually, annoyed and irritated, I reluctantly rose and fed the creature.

With my bath robe securely tied, I moved out onto the pool area, the clear water glinting in the sunshine reflecting the pure blue cloudless sky. I sipped my coffee as I slouched on the lounger, soaking up the magical atmosphere knowing that the irritations from the cat were now safely locked inside. Again, my moments were short lived, a dog began barking constantly, causing the new neighbours four dogs to join in harmony, albeit for just a few minutes before I vigorously pressed the zapper she had given me on her arrival a few weeks ago. The dogs are called Roger, Jeremy, Raymonde and Hugh and she can often be heard shouting 'Roger, stop humping Raymonde.' Things returned to normal as I relaxed and entertained myself on my iPad. Splat! the noise from hundreds of black crows could be heard overhead as I wiped the sloppy bird droppings from my iPad screen. I was reluctant to look skyward and entered the villa, making sure that the cat was evicted outside.

After lunch I went for a swim, then lay on a Lilo in the afternoon heat. Peace and tranquillity had returned but not for long. The tinkling sound of approximately one hundred and fifty goat bells could be heard from the lush field over the fence. I left the pool to watch the spectacle, they were spread out far and wide as the goat herder stood close by, puffing away on his rolled cigarette. Twenty minutes later he slowly wandered back along the track, calling out and whistling while the goats begin to follow him from all areas of the field. I find it mesmerising as the distant stragglers eventually find their way and join the rest of the herd before they disappear back to the farm.

Once again, I return to my life of peace and paradise as the sun gently browns my winter skin, but not for long. Shouting and swearing can be heard from the villa on the corner as a Cypriot father and his teenage son come head to head in an argument which disturbs the menagerie of animals they keep in a small garden with a pool. Geese, ducks and turkeys go head to head, making enough noise to disturb the whole neighbourhood while domestic rabbits hop around the bins over the road, then give a demonstration of animal re production. All this occurs many times a day.

Ah well, time for bed as I snuggle up under the duvet and wait to enter my land of fantasy and dreams, but not for long. Out of the seven local cats, two are on heat and followed round by the big boys, the gingers. The screeching and hissing in the quiet of the night, kicks off every cat in the neighbourhood, plus seven dogs and four lots of residents shouting, 'shut the f.. up.' I cover my head with the duvet and think, aah well, tomorrows another day, welcome to the island of dreams, welcome to paradise.

45) LARRY'S LAMENT

Years and years I've lived at number ten

Crapped on the floor and been booted out now and then

Caught all the mice but never a rat

They're too busy scheming for this and that

Expenses for phones, cars or a house

They take no notice when I've caught a mouse

And every day when the door opens wide

There's never any food I cried and cried

And each time I enter with a friend

The regulations drive you round the bend

Security is rife, they even frisk us

But all we want is a tin of Whiskas.

That's Rich

46) A NEW YEAR

At seventy seven, Fred Pilgrim lay on his comfy sunbed alongside his kidney shaped swimming pool. In shorts and 'T' shirt, a cool beer at hand, his favourite newspaper with crossword, the sun creating a perfect day as the rays added perfection to his already tanned muscular body.

He had been living in Cyprus which he described as paradise, for the past twelve years since his retirement from being a precision engineer for a well-known company in the U.K. The villa had been bought many years ago by him and his wife Mary to enjoy holidays away from the UK rat race but sadly she died two years later, leaving Fred to soldier on alone.

On his retirement, much to the disapproval of his family, he rented the UK house out and moved permanently to Cyprus where he had lots of friends, a great social life and most of the time, fabulous weather. Obviously, the loss of his wife had severely affected him but he knew he had to be positive and carry on, she would have expected no less from him. Compared to a lot of people his life was good. He lay back on his sunbed and thought, it's almost New Years Eve. A brand new year looms, I wonder what it will bring he mused.. Here I am, nearly the end of December, sunbathing. He finished his beer and in the warmth of the sun, dozed off. The pre new year party at a local taverna was a wonderful occasion. A superb meal with mulled wine, live music, great friends, what more to life was there he thought, apart from a nice loving partner. After a few drinks the crackers were pulled and out of Freds popped a motto, 'You have one life, you are granted one wish.' Although a bit of fun, Fred thought for a while, remembering his youth as a virile young man, out with his mates in the UK having fun, clubbing, drinking and eventually falling in love with his wife Mary. He wished to be twenty again. No sooner had he said it he tried to retract the thought as he realised what was in store, but it was too late. Suddenly he was transformed into a twenty year old. He went on a bender from pub to pub, then on to a nightclub until 2.0.am eventually crashing on his bed at 3.0.am. His alarm clock rattled his brain at 7.0.am, he staggered to the bathroom, head banging, knees weak as he threw up in the toilet. Never again, never again he thought as he held his head in an attempt to stop it spinning in a dazed incoherent state. He vomited before collapsing on the floor, sick all down his pyjamas. The alarm clock gave a second blast numbing Fred's boozed up brain. 'Shit,' he cried, I'm supposed to be at work in an hour.' He rang work to say he was sick and would not be coming in. The following day he got the sack and became another statistic at the employment centre. His girlfriend Helen, who he had known since school and who he was head over heels in love with, dumped him as she had suffered enough of his wayward life. He was heartbroken and did all he could to win her back. She too was upset but he had let her down so many times. He began to drink more and more and was often found lying in the gutter and the next day he would have no recollection of what had gone on. His debts piled up, his friends began to drift away and he was in despair, almost suicidal. He spent the cold night on a park bench, now homeless as his parents had disowned him. He pulled out the crumpled Christmas cracker motto and stared at it. Stupid bloody thing, wish I had never bothered with it, wish I was back on my sunbed in Cyprus. Feeling even more depressed, Fred drank a few large vodkas from the bottle he kept in his rucksack. In the morning he woke with a heavy head but was surprised to find he had returned to Cyprus, retired and on his sunbed by the pool. Stuff being young again he thought, nearly fifty years work in front of me, bills, stress, hangovers, stuff that. He smiled and stretched out before falling asleep in the midday sun. He woke to the sound of someone calling his

name. 'Fred, wake up, wake up.' He slowly
focussed his eyes, he barely recognised the person
standing over him but the voice and manner were
unmistakable, it was Helen, his first love. They
hugged and reminisced for the rest of the day. She
moved in with him, celebrated New Year's Eve at
a taverna with friends and retired to bed. Fred
gently kissed her on the cheek and said, 'It's
going to be a new year we will never forget; I
love you.' His life was now happy and complete.

47) THE LAST GASP

She was there, I heard her cry
She said to me, I don't want to die
She called my name, I ran to her
I held her hand, she did not stir

At six years old was I too young
To understand her worn out lung
She smoked for years, not caring why
This was the reason she was about to die

She is my nan, I love her so
I can't believe she has to go
She's been my life, my best friend
And now all this is soon to end

She's so young, it's such a shame
That she should die in so much pain
But smoking soon gets a hold
It doesn't matter if you are young or old

The last gasp, the final breath
Could be heard before her death
She gave a cough, squeezed my hand
And quickly went to another land

I gazed at her, she was not my nan
That was a story which once began
It was in my mind, back in the past,
I never heard my nans last gasp

I held the hand in front of me
And it was plain for all to see
It was not my nans but some other
Then I realised it was my mother.

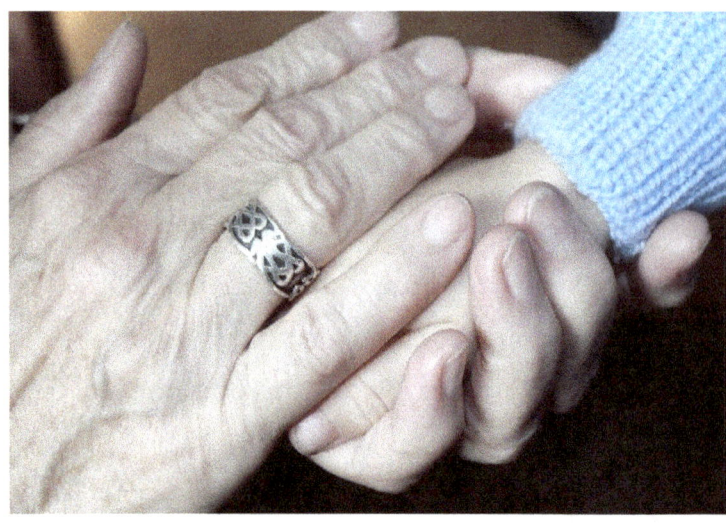

48) BRIGHT LIGHTS OF LONDON

It had taken three months to get tickets to see my favourite band at Wembley stadium. They were promised by ticket touts at a good price but then they let me down. Eventually I found them on the internet.

It was a wonderful evening along with my friend Jenny Peters. After the show we headed into the West End to see the sights and have a few drinks. As we walked passed a high class jeweller, we stopped to look at the fabulous articles which we could never afford, but a girl likes to dream. Suddenly we were attacked by five or six assailants who hit us on our face and arms. We lashed out but they just kept on coming. Two hit the shop window with force but the glass stayed intact. We ran as the other assailants turned their attention to the brightly lit shop window with its expensive goods. We jumped onto a nearby bus, thankful that we were safe.

As we entered our apartment and switched on the lights, we were again attacked by several intruders before I had chance to close the front door. We both fiercely lashed out, our arms striking wildly in a frenzied counterattack. For two slightly built girls, five foot three in height, we put up one heck of a fight. It was over in minutes; our attackers lay dead on the floor.

Breathing heavy, I looked at my friend Jenny and said, 'I'm glad that's over I hate moths.

49) UNDER ARREST

'Hello, can I speak to Mrs Angela Jones please, this is Doctor Ruthless at the hospital.'

'Yes, Mrs Jones speaking, is something wrong'

'I am sorry to have to tell you Mrs Jones, but your father has taken a turn for the worst and suffered a cardiac arrest, I suggest you attend the hospital as soon as possible.'

'Oh no,'

'What is it dear,' enquired John, her husband.

'It's dad, he's had a heart attack . . . Er, thank you doctor, we are on our way.

'I can't believe this, apart from a chest infection he was fine when I saw him yesterday, he only went in for a check-up.'

The twenty minute drive was filled with anxiety, Angela had always been close to her father until recently when things got a bit strained and a few heated arguments had occurred. Her wayward brother Dwayne had suddenly appeared on the scene after spending years in Australia following a major dispute with his father over the family business finances.

She was the sole beneficiary to her father's vast business empire as her brother had been disowned years ago but on his return her father had tried to patch things up and put his son back in the will, making him the majority shareholder.

They entered the hospital with some urgency but after a few minutes in the room, her father took his last breath and passed away.

'Typical,' said Angela, 'No sign of my useless brother, doesn't speak to dad for years, gets put back in the will but can't be bothered to turn up on his death bed.'

After various procedures and paying their respects, they left the hospital just as an ambulance with lights flashing, pulled up. The paramedics swiftly wheeled out a stretcher and pushed passed them.

'That's Dwayne,' screamed Angela as she looked at the disfigured blood stained face covered partly by an oxygen mask. 'Oh my god, what's happened.'

They followed inside but were blocked at the emergency room. 'What's happened, what's happened,' she screamed at a nurse.

'A car accident, that's all we know, please be patient and take a seat.'

Hours later they were allowed in, Angela sat on the bed. The doctor explained about the accident and that Dwayne had lost a lot of blood plus a broken leg, arm and some internal chest injuries but with operations and a lot of care, he should pull through.

He lay unconscious, breathing weakly into an oxygen mask, his head heavily bandaged, his face a mass of cuts. Suddenly the emergency alarm went off, a flurry of nurses and doctors surrounded the bed just as Dwayne took his last breath and passed away.

'What happened, why did he die, what caused his death' she asked, now shaking with the full events of the day.

The doctor replied, 'You were the cause, you have been sitting on his oxygen pipe'

The Police arrived, 'Angela Jones, you are under arrest.'

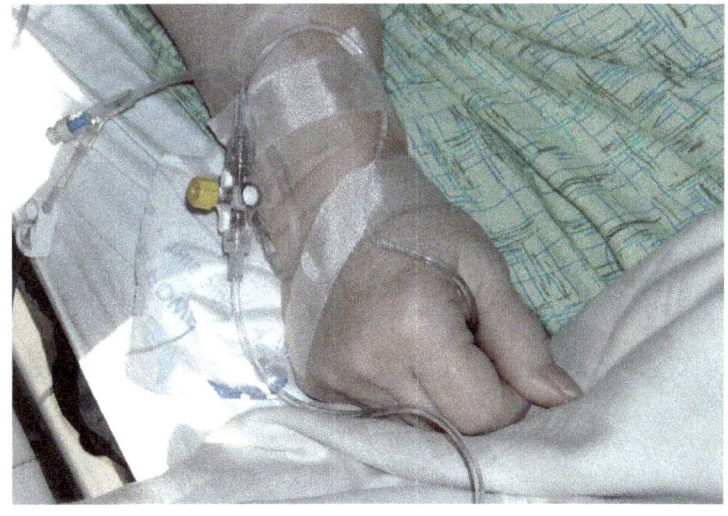

That's Rich

50) SEASICK

I used to be a sailor but it drove me out of my mind

All those days at sea, for land I struggled to find

The burning midday sun, glistening diamonds on a wave

How I longed for company, a beer I had to crave

My body grew so tired, my muscles weak and soft

As I tried to put up sails, on a mast up aloft

Bobbing up and down on the white foaming surf

How I wished for land and the feel of solid earth

I only have my memories of when I was a child

Watching golden sunsets and nature in the wild

But I was on a mission for a special cause

To help less fortunate people and open up life's doors

For this was for charity of a very special kind

For sadly now in life, I am totally blind.

51) PUSSY! PUSSY! PUSSY!

Hello, I'm just a little kitten, my name is Storm

It's been eighteen months since the day I was born

I lived on the forces base up at Episkopi

With my mum and sister who looked after me

We lived with a family who got sent away

Took my mum, not seen her since that day

Into a compound my sister 'midnight' and I were put

Mixed with other cats who around us they did strut

A big docile ginger and a nasty little grey

Who, when a cat came near, he quickly chased away

Food and drink was plenty, but I missed my mum

And when all the cats farted, the place did really hum

The staff were always smiling and each day with us they played

Looked after all our needs and made sure that we were spayed

A year went by and I decided that this was it

My home for all my life, a place to eat, play and sit

Then one day a couple came looking for a little pet

I ran around excited and grinned as we met

But my sister kept on poking in her little paws

And being almost identical, I showed her my sharp claws

But soon I was on my way to a place by the sea

A whole villa and gardens just for little ol' me

I settled in quite quickly as they gave me a gentle pat

Fed me food and water and laid out a comfy mat

But one day I got chastised for drinking a cup of tea

For I did not realise it wasn't meant for me

So now I'm very careful and watch what I sup

For now and forever I am known, as a storm in a teacup.

That's Rich

52) THE FORGOTTEN ARMY

We're on the frontline fighting a cause
Saving lives, fighting wars
And we don't need guns, rockets or tanks
And we don't need praise, just maybe thanks

Before this war we were an army lost
With government cuts at any cost
Our numbers dwindled and now we're a few
Expected to fight this war so new

An enemy out of sight
Attacking people day and night
Around the world, dropping like flies
As we hear government cries

Please help us, we need you
For we don't know what to do
But understaffed and underpaid
Lives will be lost we are afraid

So here we are fighting a cause
Saving lives, fighting wars
And we don't need guns, rockets or tanks
And we don't need praise, just maybe thanks

Our friends are dying by our side
Relatives mourning as they cried
We are struggling with this task
With the lack of gowns and a face mask

But do not worry, do not fret
Be assured this task will be met
The 'FORGOTTEN ARMY 'will sort this mess
For we are the staff of the N.H.S.

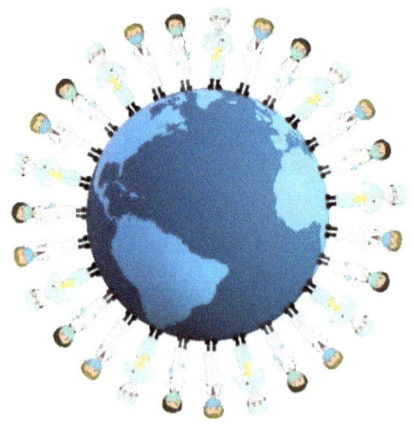

About the author

Richard Palmer was born in Stafford U.K on 6th May 1944. The second eldest of four brothers, he lived in Melling, Lancashire, a rural village a mile from Aintree Racecourse, Liverpool, until aged eighteen. He was educated at Maghull Secondary Modern School and Bootle Municipal Technical College, Merseyside. He served for eleven years in the Police Force and many years in the motor trade. His writing capabilities began at an early age with short stories, poems and newspaper articles.

After the death of his wife Barbara, aged forty-six, in 1991, he became a member of Liverpool Writers Club and produced a collection of poems. Years later, Rich and new wife Linda ran 'Firkin House', their B & B in Hoylake, Wirral, U.K, before retiring to Paphos, Cyprus in 2012. There he served as secretary of Paphos Writers Group and past co. Editor of 'The Main Sheet' newsletter at Paphos International Sailing Club, before stepping down to concentrate on his other passion, song writing.

His first book, "RICH INSPIRATIONS," Promiscuous Poems and Twisted Tales was very successful on Amazon and in Cyprus. He followed it up with "RICH IMAGINATION" and now this the third of the series.

Further information can be found on the short story and poem pages on his website,

www.thefirkinwebsite.com